# Ryme Tyme
## For Growing Minds

OUR
**30**
YEAR ANNIVERSARY

**LIMITED EDITION**

Written, Directed and Produced by

# Yusuf Ali El

*NATURAL RESOURCES UNLIMITED*
Hammond, IN 46320

# *A Special Dedication*
## *for some special boys and girls*

To my youngest Son,
## Yeshua Ali El

**To my Great grandson, Kemonte Gillenwater**
**To my Great grand-daughter, Starr Emoni Gillenwater**
**To my baby cousin, T'Mai Desire Matthews**
**To my God Daughter, Amasiah Lindo**
**To my God Son, Nehemiah Lindo**
**To Ricky's and Orly's newborn, Kamille Coffey**
**Born Sept.14, 2013**

*If there is really such a thing*
*as living on borrowed time*
*and if death came for you first*
*I would gladly lend you mine*

Little Boys
Little Girls
Little Children

Your Mothers &
Your Fathers
Love you so

We are yours
You are ours
For all the years
The weeks
The hours

From now on
For always
And ever more

To: _____

From:_____

Date:_____

A NRU Publication
Copyright ©1983, 2013 by Yusuf Ali El
All Rights reserved

Printed by United Graphics, Inc.
Printed in the United States of America
Second printing

Second Edition

Interior Art by Louise Hodges-El
Original front cover by Louis Berta
Redesign by Denise Billups, Borel Graphics
www.borelgraphics.net

Library of Congress Catalog Card Number: 83-90101

ISBN: 0-912475-09 9

# Ryme Tyme
## For Growing Minds

"*Ryme Tyme* is the first truly adequate book that will prepare the young child to develop:

1. An understanding of important academic concepts, such as counting, time, seasons, listening, categorization, and word meaning.
2. An understanding of attitude and habits which build good interpersonal and family relationships.
3. A sound foundation in positive self-worth concepts.
4. An appreciation of a rich and varied cultural heritage."

**– Dr. Beverly Normand**
President, Rald Institute

"With 10 volumes of verse to his credit, Yusuf Ali El has finally satisfied the creative requirements of his literary code of honor. "If you are a writer, until you have written for the children, you have yet to write." With the completion of his 10th and finest book, *Ryme Tyme for Growing Minds,* by his own standards, Yusuf Ali EI finally has written."

**–Nia Benyamin**
Actress

"*Ryme Tyme* is a children's book for grown-ups. The children will love it if they can get it away from their parents."

**–Tarlee Smith**

"*Ryme Tyme* is the childhood which each child deserves. Sing it; read it; color it; love it."

**–Ernestine EI**
R.N.

"*Ryme Tyme* is the lyrical score to the most beautiful children's musical to ever grace the American scene. Balladeers and folk singers can draw from its pages for generations."

**–Johnnie Haygood**
Success Thru Self Awareness

"*Ryme Tyme* is a P.M.A. manual for children. It should become the property of every parent and child."

**–Willie Bey**
Grand Sheik, HQ M.S.T. Of A.

"*Ryme Tyme* is the childhood that everyone never had. All the sting of growing up has been removed with only the sugar plums remaining. It is the most enjoyable children's book that I have ever read. Yusuf Ali EI, where have you been all my life?"

**–Ellen Beard**
Retired Headstart Dir., Chgo. Youth Center

"*Ryme Tyme* is more than just pretty words and pictures; it somehow finds and fills the niche between the ideal and the real, where happiness reigns supreme."

**–T. L. Mitchell**
Poet

"The privilege of reviewing a book as phenomenal and enlightening as Ryme Tyme only occurs once in the lifetime of a lightbearer. I am honored to be called into the sanctum of creativity, better known as the mind of 'The Poet;' Yusuf Ali EI, to witness the development of his greatest expression to date – of the Light.

There is a peace and harmony surrounding *Ryme Tyme*, every word, every stroke of the pen, every line a point of Light. The illustrations work hand-in-hand with the simplicity of the rhyme, causing an unfoldment of memories, fantasies, and dreams. Children will not only love this book – they will read it.

There's a child in every one of us who truly seeks the joys of life and the spirit of loving. Life is such a precious possession-what better way to preserve it than in song, picture, and rhyme. Yes, "Reading is a magic carpet:" I've had my ride. I think I'll have another; may you, too, enjoy your ride on this "Magic carpet" of Love. Love and Peace."

**–Ayo Maat,** Ph.D.

# Special Acknowledgements

In this cyber-paced, faster than the speed of light worlds in which we strive for meaning, it is too easy to take for granted, overlook, or just plain forget some of the VIP'S who touched and shaped our lives in some very special way.

Several people were pivotal to my writer's life. In honor of their love, I pour **literary libations.** I pour **literary libations** to Mrs. Ada Willoughby, who would not let me remain in my shell at Wilson Jr. College in Chicago, who always had time to hear and applaud my latest poems, who would not let me drop out of the University of New Hampshire because of culture shock, who arranged my first "paid" poetry reading at the recently shuttered Parkman Elementary in Chicago.

I pour **literary libations** to the late Alice Browning and her IBWC, International Black Writers Conference. *Ryme Tyme* began in a writer's workshop Alice "tricked" me into conducting at the public library on 34th and King Drive in Chicago. At Alice's invitation, I thought I was coming to recite poetry. At Alice's insistence, I found myself conducting a poetry writing workshop for some *K* to *6th grade* library visitors. I, of course, had to compose something as an example of what we were looking for and thus, my first two children's verses and *Ryme Tyme* were born. Thank you Alice Browning.

> *When it rains*
> *Little boys*
> *Go sailing ships on puddle lakes*
> *And laughing at*
> *The fun they make*
> *When......It......Rains*
>
> *When it snows*
> *Little girls*
> *Bundle up like Eskimos*
> *In their most warmest clothes*
> *When............It..............Snows*

I pour **literary libations** to Chicago's own, to the *Chicago Defender's* own, Mr. Earl Calloway. To Sister Carrie Bey. To Princess Louise Hodges-El. To Denise Borel Billups, my wonderful book designer and to Novelist Diane Martin for making the introduction. I pour **literary libations** to Mrs. Margaret Esse Danner. I pour **literary libations** to Brother Sam Greenlee, our *Spook Who Sat By The Door.*

I pour **literary libations** to: June E. DeLia, who referred the printer who printed my first two books. To Eileen Woods, who always believed. To Royer Andrews of Andrew's Printing in Harvey, Illinois. To Irvin Hawthorne of Graphic Arts Reproductions, whose scolding launched a search which brought forth Louise Hodges-El. To the Poets of Chicago Renaissance, I pour **literary libations.**

I pour **literary libations** to Ann E. Bassett. I pour **literary libations** to (Imanah) Lise Tillman-Wilson, my first literary soulmate; to Al Duckett; to Al Cain; to Hoyt Fuller of *Black World Magazine.* I pour **literary libations** to Mrs. Y. Y. Henderson and Miss Ida Lee Bush, who got me off to a great start in grades 1 through 4. Preschool and kindergarten did not exist in Pembroke, IL in those days.

I pour **literary libations** to my maternal Grandmother, Carrie Mae Herndon Randall, 1886-1965, the first poet in our family. And of course to my old fashioned stay-at-home-Mother, Bonnie Randall Mitchell. And to my old fashioned solo-bread-winner-Father, (Big Frank), Frank Lee Mitchell, who made it all possible. I pour the **literary libations** of *Ryme Tyme* unto you all.

Hotep.

**–Yusuf Ali El**
The Pembroke Poet

# Introduction

Good books are among the finest friends your child will ever know, for books are a very special brand of toy. They provide all of the unique adventure, fun, and excitement of toys, trucks, dolls, rocking horses, table games, and the myriad of cardboard, paper, plastic, metal, rubber, wood, video, imaginary and real companions which populate a child's busy world. And yet, books do something more than entertain, they also educate.

Just as authentic adulthood requires more than the mere occasion of 21 birthdays, genuine childhood requires more than the mere occasion of youthfulness.

Childhood is a special ingredient deliberately added to the lives of the young. Though every child deserves a childhood, we have but to look at the world around us to know that childhood is not to be taken for granted as is diaper rash, colic, or two sets of teeth. Childhood is an extra-added attraction, a gaily-colored tapestry of love and attention. It is a growing rain, wonderfully bestowed upon those rare children who are fortunate enough to be truly loved.

While society in general is to a large degree responsible for the welfare of its children, the main duty rests most squarely upon the shoulders of the parents. A true childhood is optional equipment in a child's life; it is an act and honor above and beyond the call of merely bringing a child into this world. While a childhood should be an inalienable right, all too often it is reserved and issued as a privilege.

"A field of weeds will grow on its own, but a garden of flowers requires cultivation." And if our children are to bloom and grow, deliberate educational stimulations must be introduced early into each child's life, that he or she might happily grow to discover and utilize their powerfully creative imaginations to a more meaningful and fulfilling degree.

Boys and girls from around the globe share their exciting worlds on the pages of **Ryme Tyme**, where ancient lands: exotic Arabia, mysterious NorthWest Amexem, wonderful Asia, Moorish America, meet and mix so perfectly with hopscotch, double-dutch, country life, city life, kites, bikes, and the likes, while never once estranging the children from complete immersion and participation in this, their new-found world of fact, friend and fantasy.

This picturesque odyssey begins where it should with light Rymes of enlightened childhoods, soft shushing bed-tyme lullabies, crinkly wake-up poems, and light-hearted songs of play. As the story flows and the adventure unfolds, it addresses the children to the beauty of family: of mothers, fathers, sisters, brothers, grandmothers, grandfathers, and great others, finally extending and over-flowing to include friends, birds, trees, clouds, pets and all of nature's many off-spring. As the pages turn, the children learn through a gentle mixture of familiar sights and sounds coupled with new and exciting things to learn. Children, just as everyone, need to have their self-esteem deliberately boosted, uplifted and reinforced through repeated exposure to life's familiar themes, as well as through the joyful challenge of meeting and mastering new words, worlds, and concepts.

We must remember that unlike many of the adult world, the constant thrust and impetus of a child's life is learning. Learning to sit-up, to crawl, to walk, talk, stand and run. Learning to tie shoes, button blouses, wrap turbans, zip trousers. Learning to open doors, answer phones, blowout matches, climb stairs. Learning to memorize, to mimic, to reason, to recognize and to question, always to question. Questions are actually your child's way of questing for knowledge. May I help cook? May I help sew? May I hold the baby? Why did you do that? Who is that? Where are we going? What's that? A child's life is one great question.

A Moorish proverb states: "Let them laugh, let them be children, for one day soon they will need some happy times to remember." A people's most vital and valuable natural resources are its children. More precious than fertile lands and great sciences, more revered than magnificent mountains and monuments, more treasured than rare stones and metals, ancient arts and artifacts, are the children of a nation. Each nationality, therefore, owes to its children and the children of the world a culture, a creed, a tangible lore, which is the embodiment of everything that is good and great about that people. The written word, delightfully illustrated is one of the finest means of fulfilling this responsibility to one's posterity and the world.

A book of his or her very own is often a child's first grown-up possession. Give them something that can last a life-time. GIVE A BOOK. Thank you, Y.A.E.

# Ryme Tyme
## For Growing Minds

*O*nce Upon a Ryme Tyme

there was a land of happy people

and all of their children were happy.

So they all made up poems and songs

about the things that made them so happy,

Once Upon a *Ryme Tyme for Growing Minds*

is Volume 1 of the story-songs

of the happy ones.

Tell me a Ryme Tyme story
Sing me a Ryme Tyme song
Read me a Ryme Tyme riddle
It won't take you long

Please sing me a song

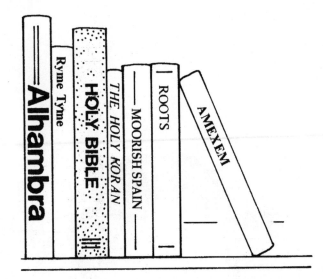

Reading is a magic carpet
Come and take a ride
The more words that you learn
The farther you can fly…

Reading is a magic carpet
Fly far as you like
From sunset poems to rainbow's end
From camelback to bike

**Reading is a magic carpet**
**And the flight is free**
    **Words are all we need to go**
    **Anywhere from A to Z...**

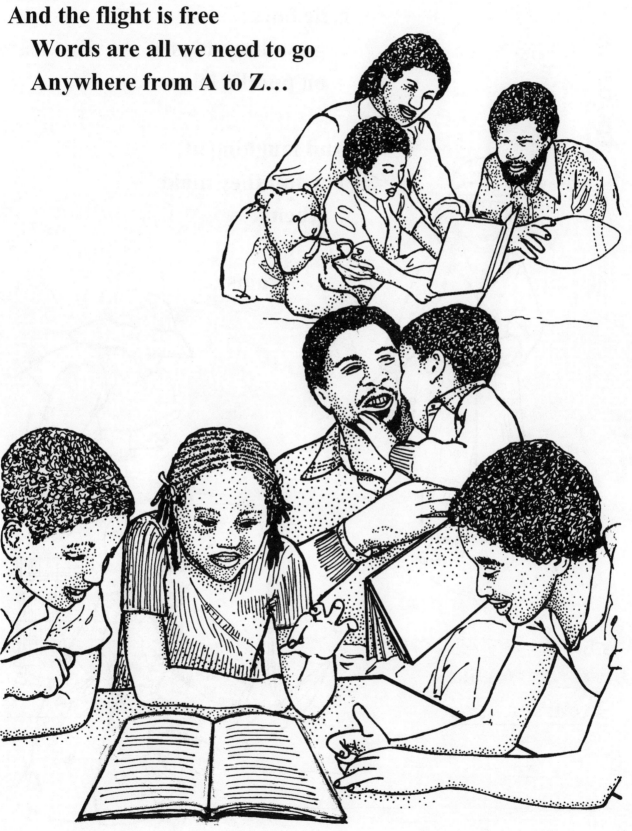

When it rains
little boys
   go sailing ships
   on puddle lakes

And laughing at
The fun they make
   when
      it
         rains…

Who makes
the rains come down
who makes
Autumn leaves turn brown

Who makes acorns
grow into oak trees
who makes the buds
grow into leaves

Who made the earth
who made the sea
who made you -&-
who made me

What is our Nationality
And who is Noble Drew Ali

What makes the breeze
blow through the trees
   What makes the flowers grow

How does the wind
make a whirl breeze spin
   What makes the rivers flow

What makes it rain
while the sun still shines
   And what makes
   a double rainbow

Let's ask Big Brother,
he'll know

If the winds
will blow for me
   may I go out and fly

My kite upon
the frisky seas
   that billow in the sky

The clouds are whitecaps
of the winds
   foaming up so high

My kite is like
a ship that sails
   the rivers of the sky

Above the trees
and chimneys
   So High
     so high
      so high

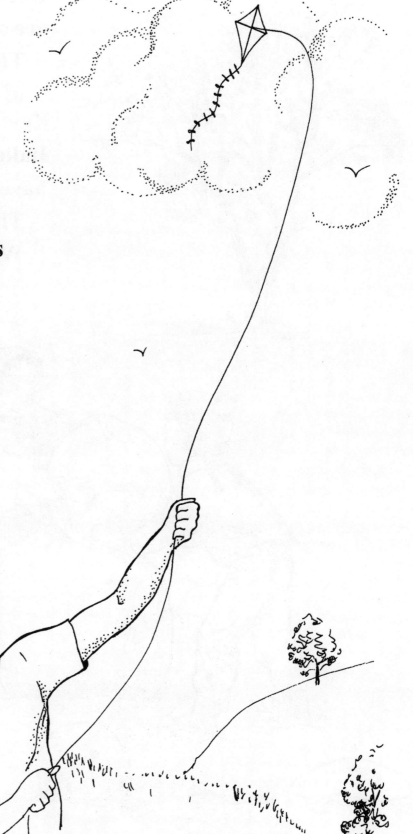

October leaves
are a'falling
  They have donned costumes
  of Autumnal gold and brown

Indian Summer winds
have come a'calling
  The leaves answer
  We'll be right down...

When it snows
little girls
  bundle up
  like Eskimos

In their most
warmest clothes
  to withstand
  the winter snows

12

The snowman is a funny man
He only likes the cold
    And if you brought him indoors
    He never could grow old...

The snowman is a funny man
He doesn't care for heat
    Jack Frost nipping at his nose
    Is really quite a treat

The snowman is a funny man
I'll tell you how I'm sure
    The colder the weather is
    The longer he endures...

The snowman is a funny man
I'll tell you how I know
    Oh he is not a real man
    He's only made of snow

That's how I know...

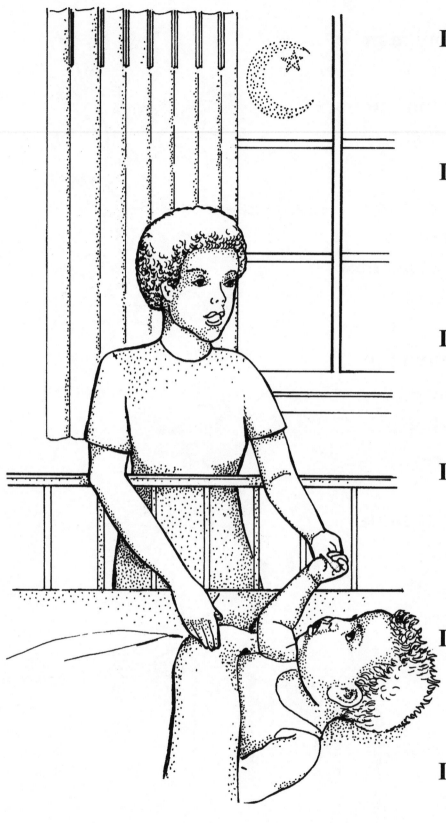

I will sing you a song
about a happy place
where the people
all live in peace
I will sing you a song
of a dream I have
a dream of the way
it will be.

I will sing you a song
of a warm sweet love
of a love that warms
the whole world.
I will sing you a song
of a beautiful place
for beautiful
boys and girls.

I will sing you a song
of a soft sweet love
of a love that grew
and grew
I will sing you a song
of a love I have
especially for you…

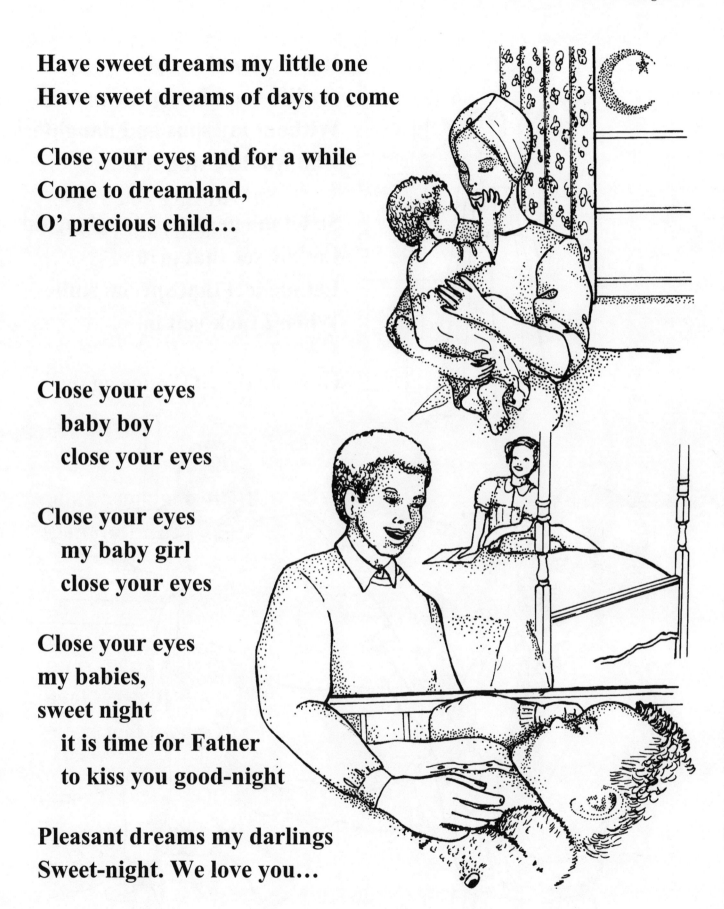

Have sweet dreams my little one
Have sweet dreams of days to come

Close your eyes and for a while
Come to dreamland,
O' precious child…


Close your eyes
  baby boy
    close your eyes

Close your eyes
  my baby girl
    close your eyes

Close your eyes
my babies,
sweet night
  it is time for Father
  to kiss you good-night

Pleasant dreams my darlings
Sweet-night. We love you…

15

If it were not for you
my life would be quite poor
Without my sons and daughters
who would I sing for

So let me hear that laugh again
Let me see that grin
Let me feel that special smile
When I tuck you in

Once again…O' once again

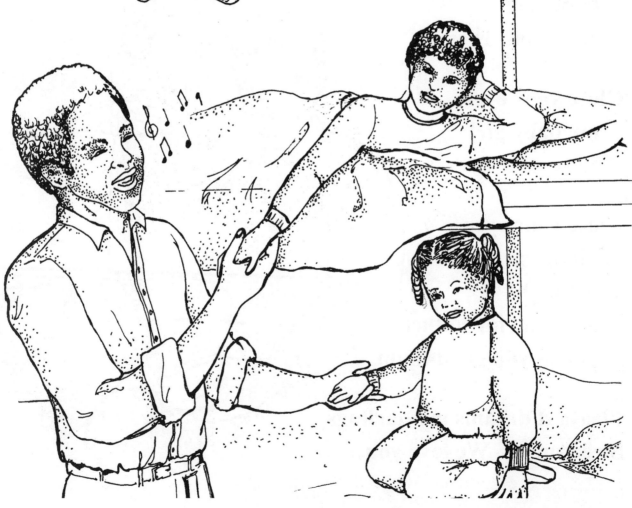

**Button black eyes**
**wrinkled feet**
    **baby-sharp nails**
    **ain't she sweet**

**Alarm clock cries**
**kicking feet**
    **Mama better hurry**
    **ain't she sweet**

**Counting little piggies**
**on baby feet**
    **all those folks**
    **saying ain't she sweet**

**All those Aunties**
**kissing little feet**
    **all those Uncles saying**
    **ain't she sweet...**

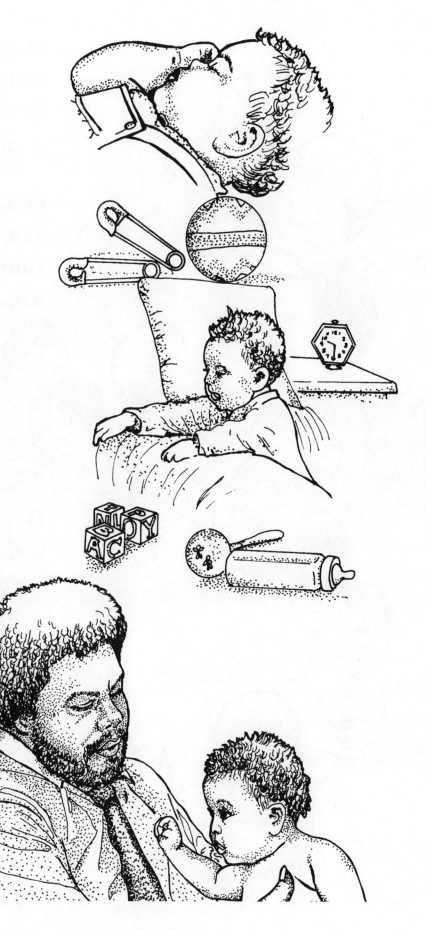

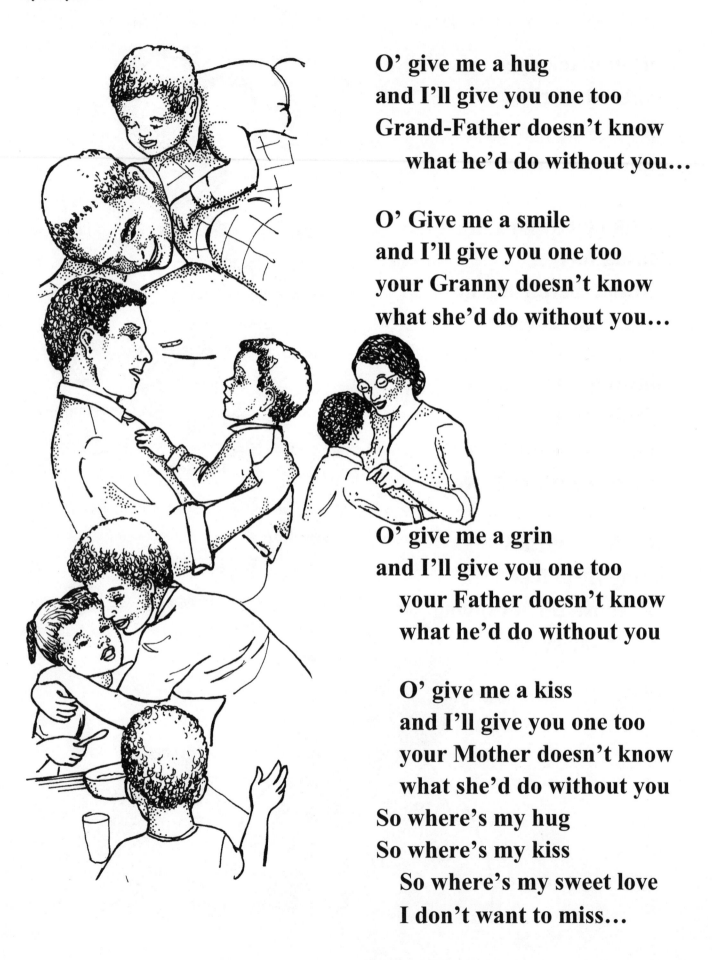

O' give me a hug
and I'll give you one too
Grand-Father doesn't know
    what he'd do without you...

O' Give me a smile
and I'll give you one too
your Granny doesn't know
what she'd do without you...

O' give me a grin
and I'll give you one too
    your Father doesn't know
    what he'd do without you

O' give me a kiss
and I'll give you one too
your Mother doesn't know
what she'd do without you
So where's my hug
So where's my kiss
    So where's my sweet love
    I don't want to miss...

So dream for me
my precious child
    go to bed
    with a smile

Knowing that nothing less
than life herself
    is very deeply
    in love with you

So dream my child
with a smile
    Allah's watching
    and I'll watch too…

…And try to remember
    whatever you dream
    and don't let it bother you

If carrots can talk
and apples have wings
    and trees can walk
    and thoughts are things

And dogs have leaves
and cats are kings
    and you're not you
    in your own dreams…

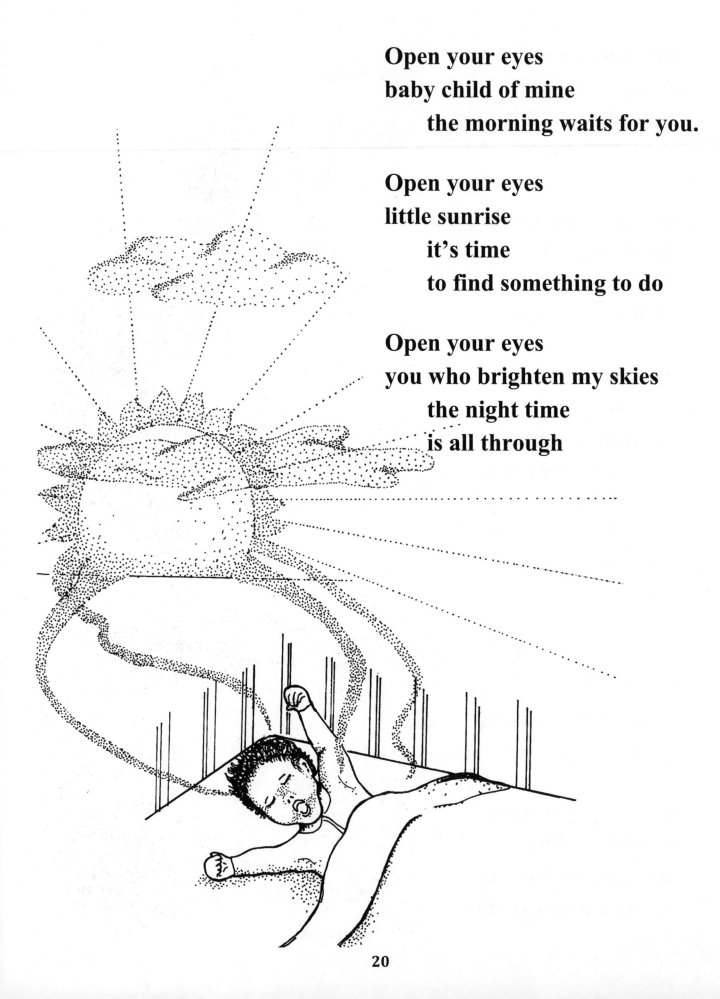

Open your eyes
baby child of mine
   the morning waits for you.

Open your eyes
little sunrise
   it's time
   to find something to do

Open your eyes
you who brighten my skies
   the night time
   is all through

**Open your eyes**
   **baby child of mine**
   **the sunshine waits for you**

**The leaves on the trees**
**the warm summer breeze**
   **are just waiting**
   **for something to do**

**The winds will not blow**
**the leaves will not float**
   **not until**
   **you open your eyes**

**The trees will not bend**
**from strong summer winds**
   **not until**
   **you meet them outside**

21

In the morning
before the rooster even crows
I slip away

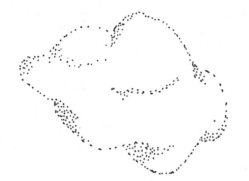

Across the pasture
through the fields
before they even hitch the plow
my toes buried in the soil
I stand and say:

I chop the weeds, feed the chickens
I tend the cows, I'm a little boy
there are a lot of things
that I can do

So I just thought I'd come and say
before I go my way
thank you for me
and a brand new day

And for the wheat fields all wet and brown
before the sun comes beaming down
and the birds all leave their nests
to search for worms

And I thank you for the eggs
that my two pullets are going to lay
and for the apples that grow
on Grandma's trees

To the east I see the sun
arising from his bed
he stretches and shakes the dew
from his sleepy eyes

And I turn back across the fields
that me and Papa are going to till
As the sun rose to warm a child's new day...

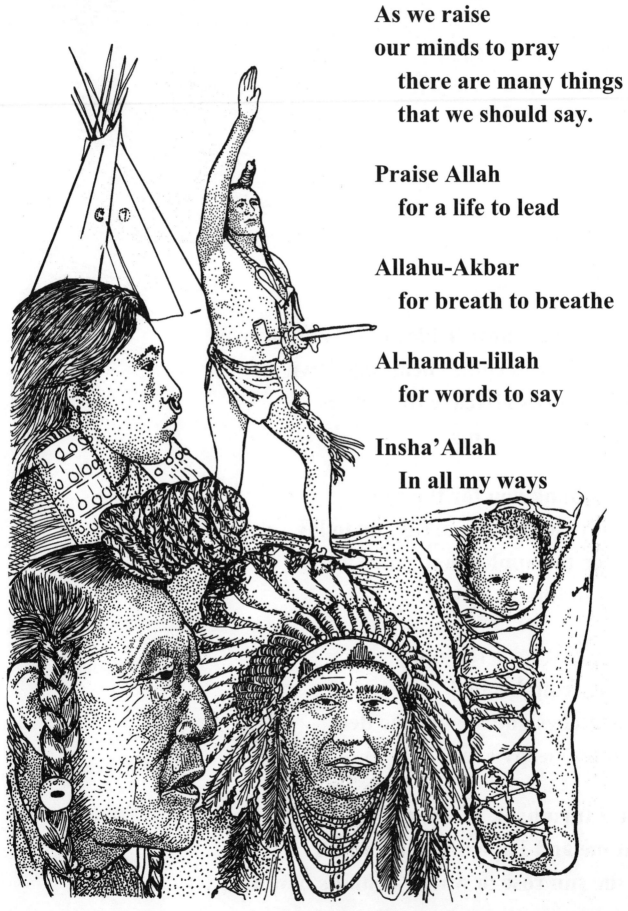

As we raise
our minds to pray
   there are many things
   that we should say.

Praise Allah
   for a life to lead

Allahu-Akbar
   for breath to breathe

Al-hamdu-lillah
   for words to say

Insha'Allah
   In all my ways

Islam Allah
Bless this day for me
and give me strength to grow

Straight and true
and loving too
in everything I think and do

Bless my Mother
Bless my Father
and Brothers and Sisters
both big and small

And my Grandparents
on both sides
and you too Allah
please bless us all

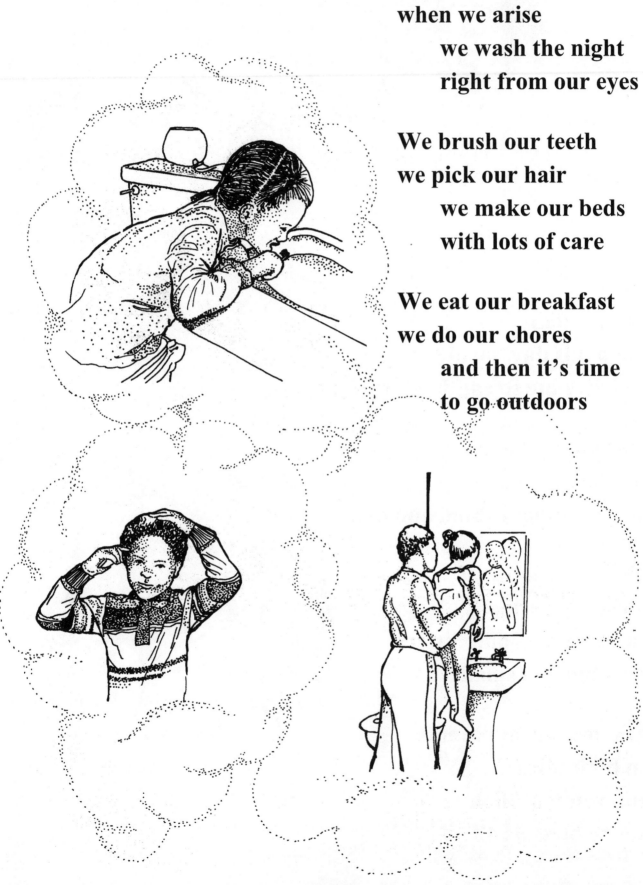

In the morning
when we arise
   we wash the night
   right from our eyes

We brush our teeth
we pick our hair
   we make our beds
   with lots of care

We eat our breakfast
we do our chores
   and then it's time
   to go outdoors

A good night's rest
a good morning's meal
   is important
   to how we feel...

Bless the food
Bless the cook
   Bless the time
   that it took

May the actions
that we take
   while strengthened
   by this food
   be always characterized
   by a loving attitude...

27

**Mother said
the other day
the art of learning
how to play**

**Is not to want
all things your way
when other children
come to play**

**Letting each one
take their turn
is the first thing
that we learn**

**That is how
we pass the day
without one fight
to spoil our play…**

**When we go
outside to play
it's double-dutch
and hide-go-seek**

**Baseball games
and froggie-leap**

**When we
go out to play…**

You get a marker
I'll get one too
   See who'll be
   the first one

   to reach Sky Blue

Oh you stepped
on the line
   won't you ever learn

   Hop-Scotch
   Hop-Scotch

   Sky Blue
   And turn…

When there's sun
there's lots of fun
   for boys and girls
   and everyone

We laugh and play
til day is done
   when
     there's
       sun…

When it's dark
we go to bed
    to have sweet dreams
    run through our heads

We hike and bike
and work and play
    until the dreams
    all go away

Then comes again
Another day...

Some tymes we play
guess who I am
we sing, we dance
we hit gland-slams

I'm Aretha Franklin
I'm Muhammad Ali

Can anyone guess
Who I might be...

Some tymes of course
A friend will come
 to join into
 my summer's fun

We run and race
and laugh and play
 until the last light
 fades away

And ends again
another day...

Hide-and-seek
Seek-n-hide
    I'm gonna getcha yet
Counting 10
once again
    here goes
    lickety-split

Everybody better run
all round my goose is it
    Counting 10
    once again
I'm gonna getcha yet
Get back… Jack…

Pitching pennies
at a sidewalk crack
    won 37-cents
    but I'll give that back

When the teacher comes
we got to run
    but that don't mean
    we ain't having fun

Ready or not
Here I come…
Here I come…

33

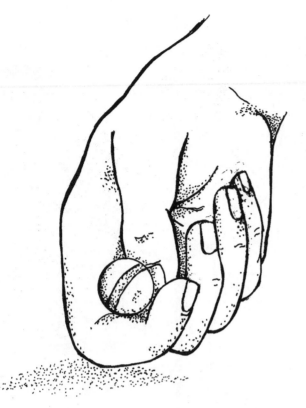

Shooting marbles
for the champeen prize
   won 6 aggies
   and 4 cat-eyes

Rolling tires
down Pembroke Road
   just passed Frankie
   now here come Joe

Playing jacks
can't get pass "One"
   but that don't mean
   we ain't having fun
   Ready or not
   Cause here I come
      Here I come…

Eating watermelon
sitting in the shade
Sweet and cold
Man I got it made

Here comes little brother
gonna want him some
But that don't mean
we ain't having fun

  Ready or not
  Cause here I come…

Skimming stones
down by the lake
Me make that
ol stone jump "8"

Brother Tom
come from behind
He make that
ol stone jump "9"

But that don't mean
we ain't having fun

Ready or not
Cause here I come
Here I come…

Ain't no fish
in the fishing hole
   Sister's feet got wet
   now she catching cold

Bumble bee come out
Freddie done got stung
   But that don't mean
   we ain't having fun

Ready or not
   Here I come
   Here I come…

37

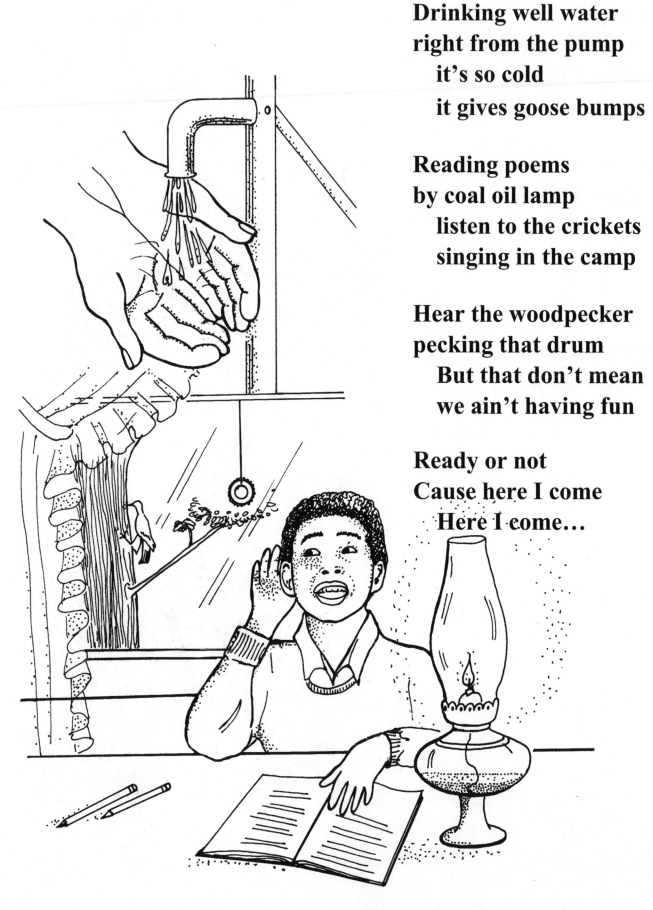

Drinking well water
right from the pump
   it's so cold
    it gives goose bumps

Reading poems
by coal oil lamp
   listen to the crickets
    singing in the camp

Hear the woodpecker
pecking that drum
   But that don't mean
    we ain't having fun

Ready or not
Cause here I come
    Here I come…

**Picking blueberries**
  **up in the woods**
**boy those berries**
  **sho' taste good**

**Come time to leave**
  **I ain't got one**
**but that don't mean**
  **we ain't having fun**

**Ready or not**
**Cause here I come**
  **Here I come…**

**The Hummingbird**
**can stand still in the air**
  **He flaps his wings so fast**
  **til he goes nowhere**

**He flaps so fast**
**til his wings just hum-mmm**

**But that don't mean**
**we ain't having fun**

**Ready or not**
**Cause here I come**
  **Here I come…**

39

I know you
yes I do
  tell by your candles
  you "3" tymes "2"

You're eating green ice-cream
eating purple cake
  you better watch out
  for Mister Belly-ache

But that don't mean
we ain't having fun

Ready or not
Cause here I come
Here I come…

1, 2, 3, on Frankie Bey
over by the shed
1, 2, 3, on Frankie Bey
no use ducking your head

1, 2, 3, on Tommie El
you can't get no free
1, 2, 3, on Tommie El
hiding by the tree

Get back
    Jack…

Who's Mother's favorite
Bet you think you know
Is it Tasha almost "9"
or Trisha turning "4"

Who's Father's favorite
bet you'll never guess
You both are the favorite
we love you both the best...

My Father knows
About everything
   like bikes
   and cars
   and broken wings

He helps me fix
My train, my skates
   and anything else
   that I might break

My Father has
just what it takes

42

He lets me sit
upon his knee
    he reads my favorite
    poems to me

He teaches things
that I should
    and lets me talk
    when it's my turn

    My Father shows
    he is concerned...

Father said to Sis and me
this knowledge is older
    than the trees

To get through life
with the greatest of ease
    remember these words

Thank you and Please...

Sometimes he takes us
to the park
  and plays with us
  til almost dark

Then we walk home
hand-in-hand
  our Father is
  the nicest man

My Mother knows
'bout lots of stuff
  like how and why
  and when and such

44

And when I'm hurt
and start to cry
    It's Mother who knows
    what dries my eyes…

She always knows
what makes me smile
    She calls me pretty
    brown dumplin' chile…

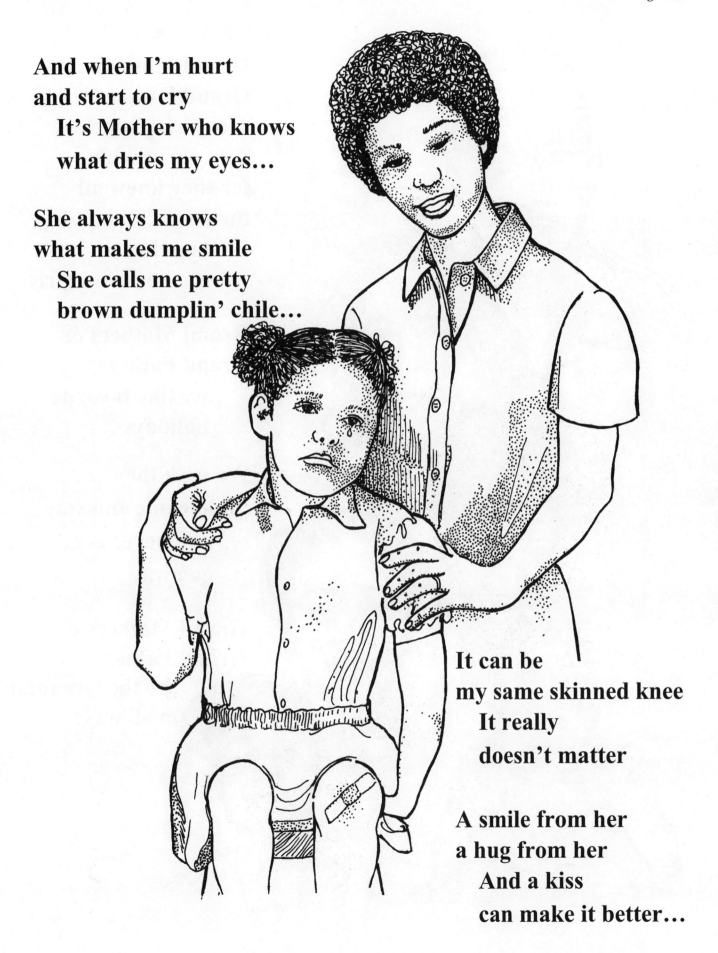

It can be
my same skinned knee
    It really
    doesn't matter

A smile from her
a hug from her
    And a kiss
    can make it better…

Grand Mothers &
Grand Fathers
    are very special
    to our worlds
for they knew all
the moms and dads
    when they
    were boys and girls

Grand Mothers &
Grand Fathers
    are like favorite
    holidays

We wish they
could come and stay
    and never ever
    go away

Grand Mothers &
Grand Fathers
    are the Grandest
    in all ways

Mother,
are grown-up tears
any easier to dry

And since big people
don't skin y'all's knees
what makes you grown-ups cry

Please tell me
Tell me why…

47

**Mamas and Papas**
**are great unsung heroes**
**whose real names nobody knows**
    **Yes, Mamas and Papas**
    **are great unsung heroes**
    **whose big scene**
    **was buttoning your coat**

**But the head-lines**
**and the big times**
    **don't give them**
    **no by-lines**
    **still they go on**
    **stealing the show**

**Yes, Mamas and Papas**
**are great unsung heroes**
    **whose big scene**
    **was wiping your nose**

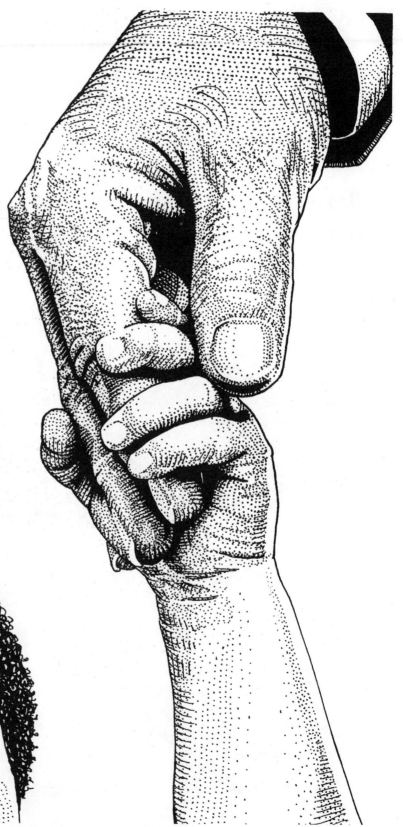

48

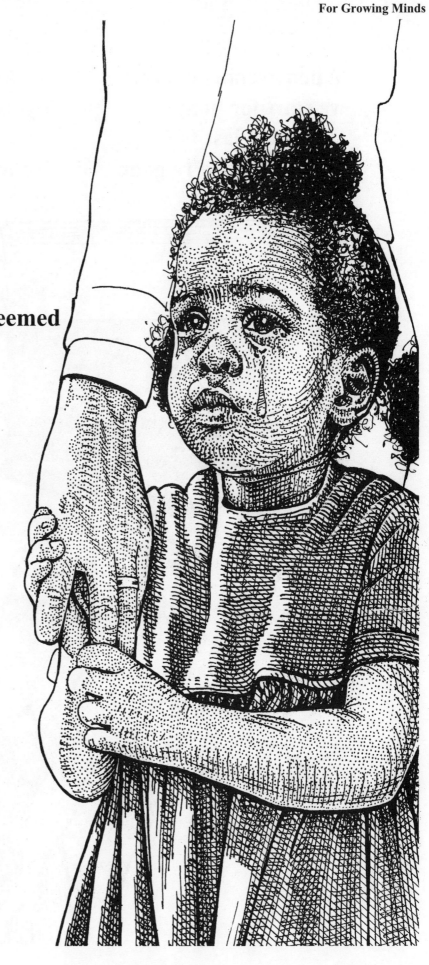

And they cried
when we cried
but their tears
   fell inside
   but that's all
   a part of the code

And they dreamed
when we dreamed
   though sometimes it seemed
   that we
   were opposite sides
   of the road

Yes, Mamas and Papas
are great unsung heroes
   whose real names
   only we know
   whose big scene
   was wiping your nose

Mama
Papa
We love You

**When evening comes
we start for home
we play last tag
and then we're gone**

**We know before
it gets too dark
we'd better be
back in our yard...**

**Brothers and Sisters
make very good friends
    Because they can stay
    when day time ends**

**And you all can play
when you come in
    When Brothers and Sisters
    are also friends...**

Back to school
is finally here
    it is my favorite
    time of year

Summer is over
school's back in
    now I can meet
    all my new friends...

Aries, Taurus, and Gemini,
Cancer, Leo, which one am I?
Virgo, Libra, and Scorpio,
Sagittarius, and away we go!

Capricorn, Aquarius,
The Pisces fish,
Oh which would you be
If you had your wish?

Earth Sign, Air Sign,
Water Sign, Fire;
Oh which would you be
If you had your desire?

Learning how
To read and write
   is the thing
   that I most like

Learning how
To count and spell
   is something I like
   just as well

Words and numbers
everywhere
   if you can read
   you can go there

53

What tyme is it
what tyme is it
   O what tyme can it be
The skinny hand
is on the "12"
   the fat hand
   is on "3"...

What tyme is it
what tyme is it
   it's tyme for me to go
The small hand
is on the "9"
   the big hand is on "4"...

What tyme is it
what tyme is it
   can anybody tell

The short hand
is on the "6"
   the long hand
   is on "12"

What tyme is it
what tyme is it
remember what Father said

When both hands
are on the "9"
it's tyme
we were in bed…

What tyme is it
what tyme is it
it's later
than it seems

When both hands
are on the "10"
its tyme
for us to dream

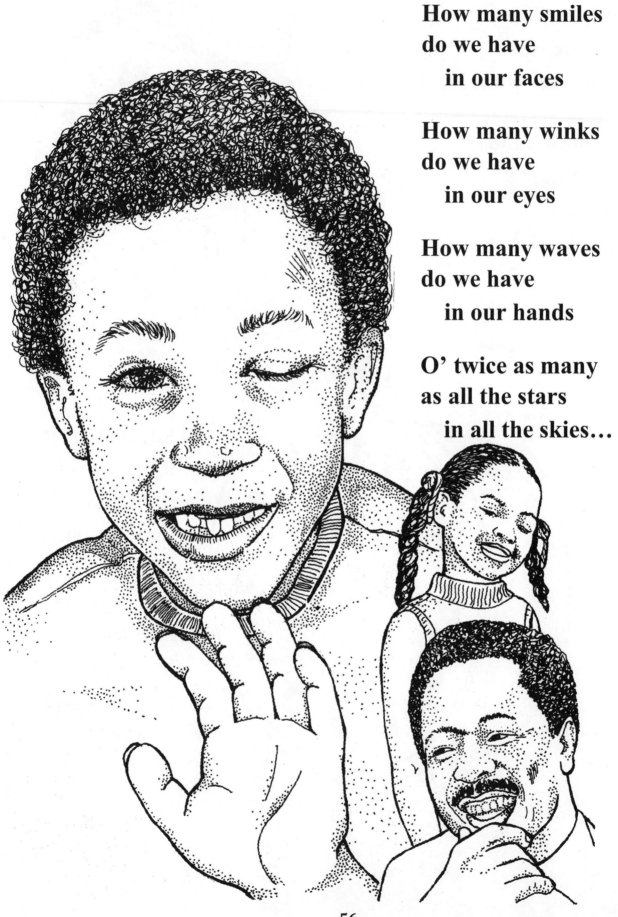

How many smiles
do we have
    in our faces

How many winks
do we have
    in our eyes

How many waves
do we have
    in our hands

O' twice as many
as all the stars
    in all the skies...

56

Robins come
from speckled eggs

Syrup comes
From Maple runs

Sisters come
From the Plane of Love

But from where
Do Brothers come

Fathers
Talk to your sons…

How does the squirrel
know which hole
    to go in

How does the Robin know
in which tree
    to build her nest

How do the leaves
know when to dance
    for the whirlwind

And how does the Dove know
which of her songs
    we like best
Can you
Can you guess?...

Every dream
must start somewhere
  and somewhere
    is right here

Some dreams are born
on mountain tops
    some on
      the open plains

  Yet anywhere
  a dream begins
    is really quite the same

For dreams begin
within the heart
    with things
      that eyes can't see

And there are dreams
just waiting
to begin
with you and me

If we only
let them be...

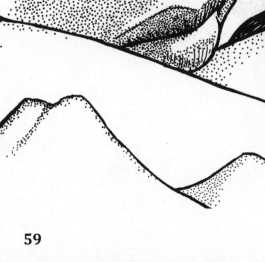

59

**Climbing trees**
**is always fun**

**I find and climb**
**the tallest ones**

**And look the sky**
**right in the eye**

**I like tall trees**
**Do you know why…**

Sometimes I wish
I were a bird
    flying high
    up in the sky

Sometimes I wish
I were a cloud
    so flowers could grow
    where I cry

Sometimes I wish
I were a ship
    out sailing
    the high seas

But most of the time
I'm just glad
    just glad
    that I'm just me...

In my garden
guess what I grow
   sweet corn
   crowder peas
   carrots by the row

In my garden
guess what I'm planning
   pole beans
   collard greens
   and blueberry canning...

In my garden
guess what I grow
   swiss chard
   string beans
   cabbage by the row

In my garden
guesss what I'm planning
   sugar beets
   candied sweets
   and cucumber canning...

A field of grass
birds flying o'erhead
and here alone I lie
   watching the clouds
   with their many faces
   go rolling slowly by

Their changing shapes
they come to me
   fantasies
   of believing eyes

I marvel
as children run and tumble
   on soft cushions
   of the skies

The sky's roof
of blues and whites
earth's floor
an Autumn brown

The sun's rays
flecks of here-after
come floating
gently down

But comes the time
I must start home
my imprint
it stays behind

And the calm serenity
that I just knew
it stays
upon my mind...

**Winter is
the tyme of snow...**

**Spring makes flowers
bloom and grow...**

**Summer brings
the warmest days...**

**Autumn makes
the leaves all change**

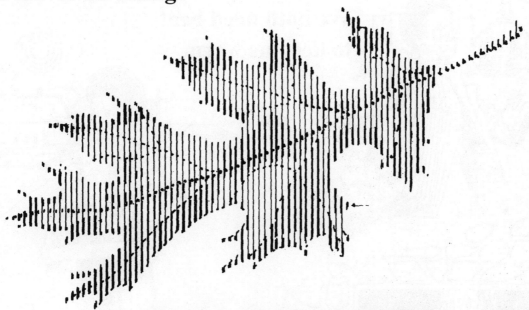

**Moorish (Indian) Summer
encores warm winds**

**And then it's Winter
once again**

I live in the city
I live on the farm
We both need heat
to keep us warm

I skate on a pond
I skate on a rink
We are really quite
alike we think

I climb trees in the park
I climb trees in the woods
Climbing trees
is really good

I swim in the river
I swim in the pool
We think swimming
is really cool

I ride my scooter
I ride my bike
We think we all
are quite alike…

When I grow up
When I grow up
   I wonder
   what I'll be

Musician, Poet, or Painter,
Explorer, King, or Queen…

When I grow up
When I grow up
   I wonder
   what I'll be

With all the world
to learn about
   and all the world
   to see

I wonder
what I'll be

If I could
    Back in time I'd go
        To Ancient Egyptland

And with my own eyes
    See who stood
        The Pyramids on sand

Then off I'd go
    From Morocco
        To lend a helping hand

To extend the Arts
    And Sciences
        And Destinies of Man...

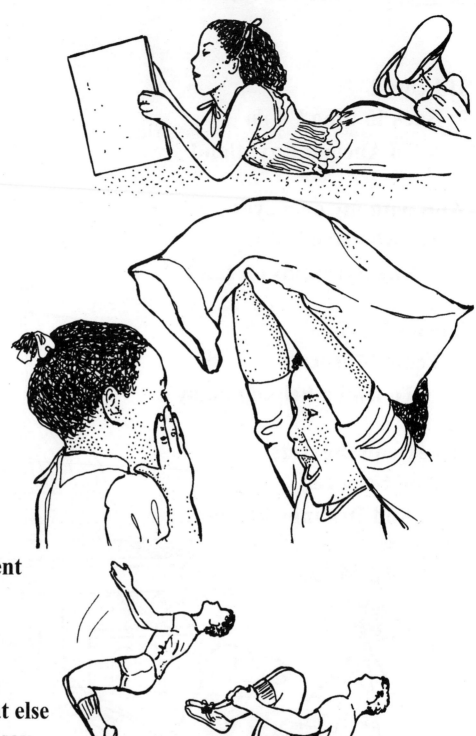

Childhood dreams
and phantasies
   constantly
   reminding me
   of how
   it used to be

Bed-tyme stories
nursery rymes
   lights out
   and last one in
   are playing tag
   inside my head

Pillow fights
and blanket tents
   good-night kiss
   and prayers all sent
   come calling me
   to yesterday

   And I declare
   I don't know what else
   this poem should say

Somersaulting
sidewalk games
   just like the ones
   children still play
   are taking place
   inside my brain…

Hide-go-seeking
see-saw times
   are hop-scotching
   through my mind
   again today

**And I declare**
**I don't know what else**
   **this song should say**
   **this song should say**

**If I gave each of you**
**15 minutes to think of all**
   **the games that you could…**
**When the time was up**
**you would still be thinking**

   **Because running fast is a game**
   **And not being last is a game**
   **And Root-the-Peg is a game**
   **And last tag is a game…**

**And when I would tell you**
**that your time was up**
   **you would be saying…**

**Oh, how could I forget…**

**Boyfriend, girlfriend**
**grade school crush**
   **puppy love**
   **first kiss**
   **first blush**
   **first grown-up tears**

**Just yesterday's**
**remember whens**
   **do you recollects**
   **and way back thens**

   **come crowding in**
   **like childhood play…**

**And I declare**
**I don't know what else**
**Ryme-Tyme should say**
**Ryme-Tyme should say...**

74

**Love** lives in
the river's flow
Love lives in
the good we know

**Truth** lives in
the sun that shines
Truth lives in
the child that's kind

**Peace** lives in
the flowers and trees
Peace lives in
the airs we breathe

**Freedom** lives in
free winds that blow
Freedom lives in
free love we show

**Justice** lives in
sweet songs we sing
Justice lives in
just everything

Kwanzaa comes near Christmastide
and lasts for seven days

To bring the Seven Principles
to guide us in our ways

From December twenty-six thru January first
We celebrate the Principles
which bring us "Peace On Earth"

As each day progresses the celebration thrives
Bringing precious meaning to our complicated lives

The gifts are Sacred words given in a special way
Seven Special Principles – one to mark each day

Umoja means Unity
Working as one throughout the land

Kujichagulia means self determination
The Hallowed fundamental Principle
of every woman, child and man

Ujima means collective work and responsibility
All for one, one for all, til we all are free

Ujamaa means cooperative economics
Pooling positive resources,
Cooling negative comments

Nia means purpose

Kuumba means C-R-E-A-T-I-V-I-T-Y

And Imani depicts the Faith we have
In these Principles to keep us free

# Nguzo Saba

And I declare
I don't know what else
Ryme-Tyme should say
Ryme-Tyme should say…

# About the Author

Yusuf Ali EI, Moorish American Master Poet and story teller, was born to Frank and Bonnie Mitchell El on the 8th of March, 1948, while the sun was in Pisces.

City born, but country bred, Yusuf grew up on a farm in rural Pembroke Township, Illinois. As a child, in addition to his brothers, Frankie and Tommie, young Ali El's earliest companions were the pheasants, squirrels, rabbits, bull snakes, tadpoles, frogs, crows, robin red-breasts, turtles, quail, oak trees, acorns, barnyard creatures and the countless creeping and crawling many legged creatures who shared the rustic countryside.

In a sense, *Ryme Tyme* is those early years. "On the way to school," Ali EI reports, "during different times of the year, we could stop along the way to partake of the blueberries, blackberries, and huckleberries which grew in all the woods. If we left home early enough we could stop by Mrs. Annie Johnson's plum trees, Mr. Riddle's apple trees, Mr. Edward's cherry trees or conduct a friendly raid on John Farney's yellow-meat watermelon patch which grew almost undetected in one of his many corn fields.

Early autumn found us foraging for the wild tangy grapes which grew in abundance along the dredged stream which paralleled the Howard's Road. So tart were they, til our mouths would sometimes sting for hours from our culinary abandon and youthful over indulgence.

The fullness of Fall brought forth the hazelnut, and the pungent sassafras roots which were dug and used for winter teas. Fall also brought forth another treat. After the farmers harvested their corn, we could go forth into the still fruitful fields and glean, much as Ruth, our Moabitess Sister had done thousands of years earlier.

Two bushel baskets of corn, or one croaker sack full fetched a handsome 75¢ from the locals who had either not enough land to grow their own or not enough time to glean for themselves. As I think back on it though, another strong possibility vies for eminence. They bought our corn to encourage and reward the industrious natures of the children of the countryside. Just as today, I hire a neighborhood lad to do what I can easily do myself.

Winter rewards were measured in snowmen, snowangels, snowball skirmishes, snow-sledding and snow-cream recipes of fresh snow, Milnot cream, vanilla extract and sweetened to taste. This extravagant dessert was then placed on the roof of our house trailer to freeze into a delicious after supper delight."

Yusuf's true education was growing up in the country, studying by kerosene lamp, using outhouses, pumping water out of the ground, walking several miles to school and knowing that life was not dependent upon electricity. His "formal" training was by a more standard route.

He attended Gobin Elementary School in Leesville, Ill., Pembroke Consolidated, (A.KA.) Lorenzo Smith School in Hopkins Park, Ill., St. Anne H.S. in St. Anne, Ill., and graduated from Wendell Phillips H.S. in Chicago, Ill.

He continued his formal training at several colleges and universities. Yusuf earned his A.A. degree from Wilson Junior College, aka Kennedy-King, his B.A. from the University of New Hampshire, his Masters in Language and Literature from Governors State University and his Nationality Degree from the world renown Moorish Science Temple of America.

Yusuf Ali-EI, Founder-Publisher of the Natural Resources Unlimited and Chicago Renaissance of America, says, "Anyone interested in the world of tomorrow who ignores the children of today, has no future as of right now."

# Natural Resources Unlimited
## New Releases

*Raw Tears*
(Relationship Poetry, 196 PAGES), December 2011

*How To Feel Good About Yourself*
(Motivation Manual, 72 PAGES), July 2013

*Ryme Tyme for Growing Minds*
(Children's Illustrated Book, 94 PAGES), October 2013

*Thank You -&-Please*
(Children's Illustrated Social Etiquette Book, 44 PAGES), December 2014

*One Room Shack*
(Relationship Poetry) 40th Anniversary Limited Edition, December 2013

*O Woman*
(Relationship Poetry), 40th Anniversary Limited Edition, January 2014

*Tapestry*
(Relationship Poetry), 39th Anniversary Limited Edition, March 2014

Preview current publications at:
**www.rawtears.com**

*To contact Yusuf Ali EI write:*
*P.O. Box 1387 Hammond, IN. 46325*
*or via email:*
**yusufaliel@gmail.com**

*or Twitter:*
**@Yusuf_thePoet**

natural resources unlimited

NRU

incorporated